To Max —MB

For Victor —GP

VIKING
An imprint of Penguin Random House LLC, New York

First published in the United States of America by Viking,
an imprint of Penguin Random House LLC, 2021

Visit us online at penguinrandomhouse.com.

LIBRARY OF CONGRESS CATALOGING-IN-PUBLICATION DATA IS AVAILABLE

Manufactured in China

ISBN 9780593114018

10   9   8   7   6   5   4   3   2   1

Book design by Greg Pizzoli and Jim Hoover   Set in Clarion MT Pro

LEVEL 1:

KID RAD

Oh. Looks like rain.

On rainy days like today,
do you know what is nice?
It is nice to stay in
and read a good book!

The Lady sits in her chair.

Rex jumps up with her.

Jack! Quick! Come in!
It's a good day to read!

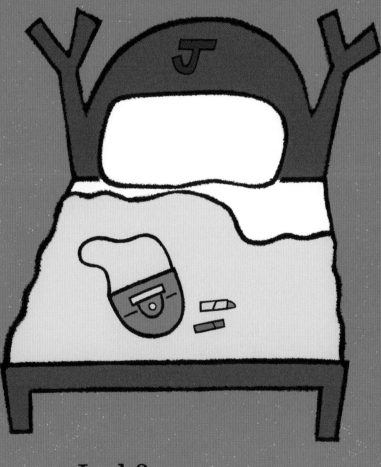

Jack?
Where is Jack?

Jack is playing a game.

A game called Kid Rad.

Jack, do you want
to turn off your game?

To sit by the fire
and read a good book?

In this book,
a king shares
his gold with
a dragon!

In this book,
teamwork
makes the
moon safe!

In this book,
a rude kid
learns to say
please!

I bet your game does not
have cool stuff like that!

OK, Jack.

LEVEL 2:
ZAP!

The Lady and Rex
curl up with a book.

Jack sits and
plays games.

The rain falls.

And then—

Where is Jack?

Oh no!

This is bad.

LEVEL 3:

IN THE GAME

Wow. Jack got zapped.
Zapped into the game.

He lives in the game now.
Jack! You are trapped!

Oh. Jack seems glad.

Jack jumps up
and smashes a block.
A coin pops out.

Jack does a dance.

He hops over a pit.
Then he does a dance.

He stomps on a bad guy.
And then does a dance.

OK! This is fun!

Where will we go next?

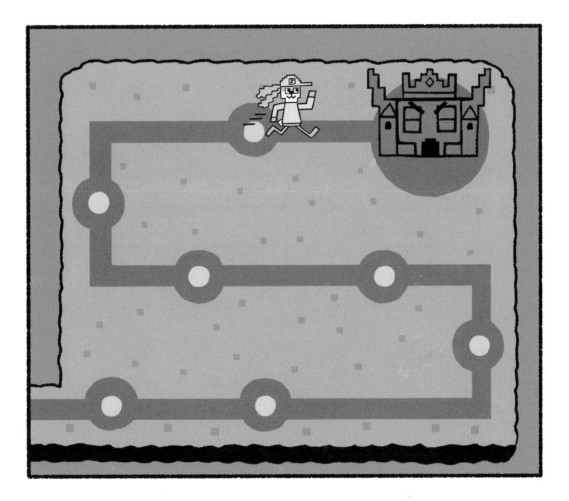

Cool!

To the Boss Base!

LEVEL 4:

BOSS BATTLE

Jack sneaks into the base.

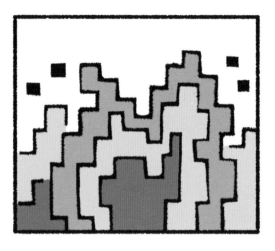

There is a fire.

Quicksand.

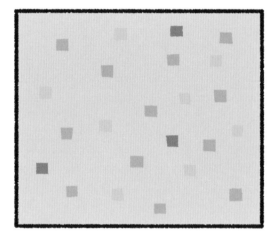

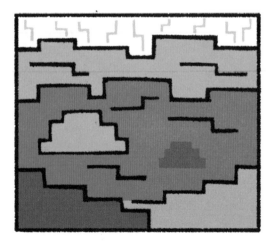

There is
hot lava.

Oh! This is rad!

Jack hops over them all
and then does a dance.

Look! There is the Boss!

The Boss is big!
The Boss looks mean!
How will you
beat the Boss, Jack?

The Boss grabs Jack!
Oh no!

You lose, Jack!

So.

Who can save Jack?

LEVEL 5:

PLAYER 2

"Fine," says the Lady.
"Let's see how this works."

The Lady hits START.
She hits A.
She hits B.

She hits UP.
She hits DOWN.

She plays as Kid Rad!

OK!

Now break that
block for a coin!

Oh.

Kid Rad just sat.

Um. Hit A.
Hit A to jump.

There you go! Yeah!

You got this! Now go!
Hop over that pit!
Press A and RIGHT!

Oh.

You fell in.

That's OK!

You get three lives.

So you have two lives left!

Just stomp on this
bad guy and—

You died again.

LEVEL 6:

LAST
LIFE

OK. Well.
You have just
one life left.

LIVES . . . 01

So don't die again.
You have to save Jack.

Sneak into the base.

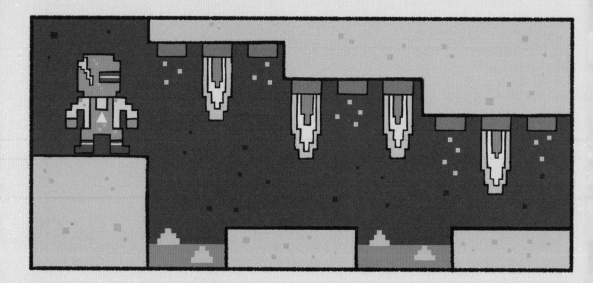

Duck under that fire.

Block that lava blast.

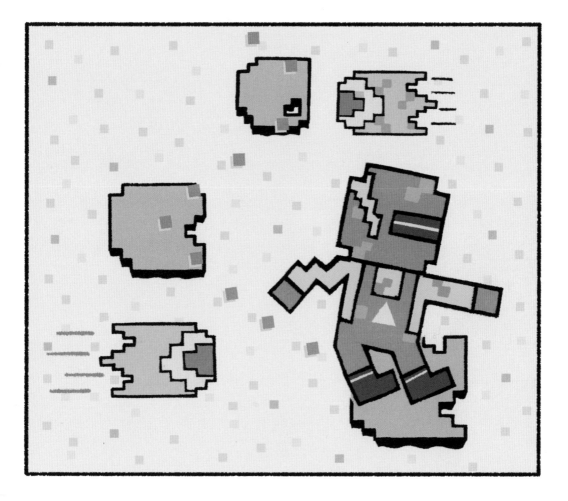

Hop over that quicksand.

Now climb up to the top.

There's
the Boss.

And
there's
Jack.

The Boss shoots
fire out of its mouth.

The Boss blasts
rays out of its eyes.

The Boss pounds the
ground with its big fist.

Oh. I hope you
are ready for this.

Hit A! Hit B! Hit A!
Three times! Fast!

Now UP!
Now DOWN!
Now hit B again!
A! B!
Down! Up! Left!
Right!
Down! A!
Smash B!
Smash A!
Smash A and B!
Yes!

Good! Now you have to
stomp the Boss on the head.

Jump down and stomp!

Go! Go, Kid Rad!

SMASH!

Yes! You did it!
You win!

You beat the Boss!
You saved Jack!

Kid Rad takes off her mask.

She and Jack do a dance.

The Lady throws up her hands.

She screams and laughs.

The rain beats down
on the house

and then . . .

ZAP!
Lights off!

Lights on!

Jack got zapped back!

Rex licks
Jack's face.

The Lady
hugs Jack.

What a day!
Oh. It's night.

A lot of time passed!

LEVEL 7:

WARM BEDS

On rainy nights like tonight,
do you know what is nice?

It is nice to sleep
in a warm bed!

Look!
There is Jack,
asleep in his bed.

And look, there is Rex.
Rex is in bed.

Good night, Rex!
Good night, Jack!
Have a nice rest!

And good night, Lady!
Wait. She's not in her bed.

It is so late!
This makes no sense.
Lady, where are you?

Oh.
Turn it off.
Go to bed.

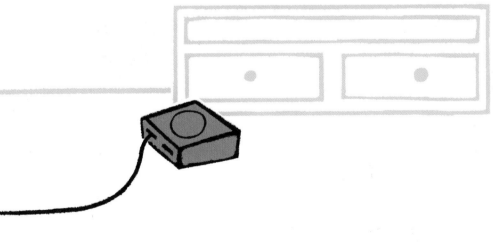

HOW TO DRAW...
ZAPPED JACK!

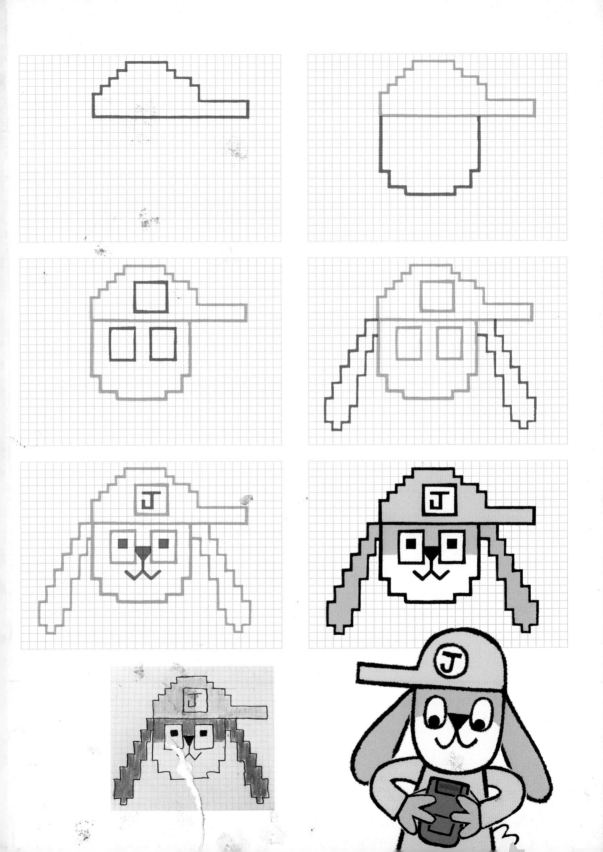

IF YOU WANT MORE JACK, READ: